# YASMIN
## The Friend

written by
SAADIA FARUQI

illustrated by
HATEM ALY

PICTURE WINDOW BOOKS
a capstone imprint

To Mariam for inspiring me, and Mubashir
for helping me find the right words—S.F.

To my sister, Eman, and her amazing girls,
Jana and Kenzi—H.A.

Yasmin is published by Picture Window Books, an imprint of Capstone.
1710 Roe Crest Drive
North Mankato, Minnesota 56003
www.capstonepub.com

Text copyright © 2020 by Saadia Faruqi.
Illustrations copyright © 2020 by Capstone.

Library of Congress Cataloging-in-Publication Data is available on
the Library of Congress website.
ISBN: 978-1-5158-4644-4 (hardcover)
ISBN: 978-1-5158-5888-1 (paperback)
ISBN: 978-1-5158-4649-9 (eBook PDF)

Summary: Yasmin knows exactly what she wants to play when her
friends come over. But it turns out her friends have their own ideas.
Could a creative compromise make everyone happy?

Editorial Credits:
Kristen Mohn, editor; Lori Bye and Kay Fraser, designers; Jo Miller,
media researcher; Tori Abraham, production specialist

Design Elements:
Shutterstock: Art and Fashion, rangsan paidaen

Printed in the United States of America.
PA100

# TABLE OF CONTENTS

Chapter 1
GUESTS.................................................... 5

Chapter 2
A FIGHT BETWEEN FRIENDS.................10

Chapter 3
A NEW GAME..........................................16

## CHAPTER 1

# Guests

Yasmin was excited. Ali and Emma were coming over to play.

"I want to have a perfect day," she told Baba. "I will plan lots of fun things to do and yummy snacks to eat."

"Sounds great," Baba agreed. "But don't forget to ask your friends what they would like to do. Friends are a blessing. We should make them happy."

Yasmin brought her box of dress-up clothes into the living room. "We're going to have so much fun!" she sang.

Ali arrived first. He had a bag

of small balls with him. "I'm

learning to juggle," he said.

"You didn't have to bring

your toys," Yasmin said to Ali. "I

have lots of things to play with."

Then Emma arrived. She held up a new jump rope. "My uncle gave this to me for my birthday," she said. "Isn't it neat?"

# CHAPTER 2

# A Fight Between Friends

Yasmin opened her box of costumes. She held up a unicorn suit.

"Let's play dress up," she said. "Nani made these costumes for me. What do you want to wear?"

Ali headed for the backyard.
"Nah! I want to juggle. I'm going
to be a famous juggler when I
grow up."

Yasmin frowned. She and
Emma followed Ali outside.

They watched as Ali tossed
the balls in the air. One by one
they landed on the ground.

One hit him on the nose.

"Ha!" Emma laughed. "You
need lots of practice."

She started to jump rope.

"Yasmin, count how many times
I can jump."

Yasmin shook her head.

"But I want to play dress up," she complained.

She didn't think Ali and Emma were being very good friends.

Ali crossed his arms over his chest. "I don't want to jump rope or play dress up. I'd rather juggle."

Yasmin watched as her
friends played by themselves.

Ali juggled by the bushes.

Emma jumped rope. "One,
two, three, four!"

Yasmin groaned. Why didn't
anyone want to play dress up
with her?

# CHAPTER 3

# A New Game

Baba helped Yasmin make a tray of snacks. There were cookies and gajar to eat. There was mango lassi to drink.

"I'm sure they'll fight over what to eat too," Yasmin grumbled.

Baba patted Yasmin's shoulder. "Remember to think about what your friends want. Not just what you want, jaan."

Yasmin looked out the window at Emma and Ali.

*How can I get my friends to play*

*together?* Yasmin wondered.

Two squirrels jumped over

one another, carrying acorns.

Yasmin's eyes grew big.

"I have an idea!" she shouted.

"What's your idea?" Baba
asked.

"You'll see!" Yasmin said and
ran outside.

"Let's play Juggle Jump!"

Yasmin said to Emma and Ali.

Emma stopped jumping.

"How do you play that?"

"We jump rope while juggling

balls. We count how many times

we can each jump," Yasmin

explained.

"Sounds fun," Ali said.

"Bonus points if you wear a

costume!"

They took turns twirling the
rope and juggling and jumping.
It was so much fun!

Soon they fell down on the grass, laughing.

Baba came outside with the tray.

"Snacks!" the kids cheered. "Thank you!"

"Juggle Jump was a great idea, Yasmin," Ali said while they ate.

"Yes!" Emma agreed. "It's more fun when friends play together!"

# Think About It, Talk About It

* What games do you like to play with your friends? What activities do you like to do when you're playing by yourself? How is it different to play with a friend or by yourself?

* Yasmin's baba says that friends are a blessing. What do you think he means by this?

* What are some ways you can be a good host when you have friends over? How do you like to be treated when you are at a friend's house?

# Learn Urdu with Yasmin!

Yasmin's family speaks both English and Urdu. Urdu is a language from Pakistan. Maybe you already know some Urdu words!

**baba** (BAH-bah)—father

**gajar** (GAH-jer)—carrots

**hijab** (HEE-jahb)—scarf covering the hair

**jaan** (jahn)—life; a sweet nickname for a loved one

**lassi** (LAH-see)—yogurt drink

**mama** (MAH-mah)—mother

**nana** (NAH-nah)—grandfather on mother's side

**nani** (NAH-nee)—grandmother on mother's side

**salaam** (sah-LAHM)—hello

**shukriya** (shuh-KREE-yuh)—thank you

# Pakistani Fun Facts

Yasmin and her family are proud of their Pakistani culture. Yasmin loves to share facts about Pakistan!

## Location

Pakistan is on the continent of Asia, with India on one side and Afghanistan on the other.

Islamabad

PAKISTAN

## Population

Pakistan's population is more than 200,000,000 people. It is the world's sixth-most-populous country.

## Fun and Adventure

In Pakistan, soccer (called football) is a popular sport among boys and girls.

The first Pakistani to have traveled to the North and South Poles is a young woman named Namira Salim.

# Make a Plastic Bag Jump Rope

SUPPLIES:
- 10–12 used plastic bags of different colors
- scissors
- duct tape

Steps:

1. Cut the bags open and lay them flat.

2. Cut the handles off so that each bag is a large, rectangular piece.

3. Cut each rectangle into several strips of plastic.

4. Tie the strips together end-to-end to make a long plastic rope. Make it slightly longer than you'd like your jump rope to be.

5. Repeat this until you have 9 long, colorful ropes.

6. Tape the ends of 3 of the ropes together. Then braid the ropes. Tape the other ends together when done. Repeat this process with the other ropes to make 3 braids total.

7. Now braid the 3 braided ropes together into one strong rope.

8. Wrap the ends in duct tape to make handles for the jump rope.

Saadia Faruqi is a Pakistani American writer, interfaith activist, and cultural sensitivity trainer previously profiled in *O Magazine*. She is editor-in-chief of *Blue Minaret*, a magazine for Muslim art, poetry, and prose. Saadia is also author of the adult short story collection, *Brick Walls: Tales of Hope & Courage from Pakistan*. Her essays have been published in *Huffington Post*, *Upworthy*, and *NBC Asian America*. She resides in Houston, Texas, with her husband and children.

Hatem Aly is an Egyptian-born illustrator whose work has been featured in multiple publications worldwide. He currently lives in beautiful New Brunswick, Canada, with his wife, son, and more pets than people. When he is not dipping cookies in a cup of tea or staring at blank pieces of paper, he is usually drawing books. One of the books he illustrated is *The Inquisitor's Tale* by Adam Gidwitz, which won a Newbery Honor and other awards, despite Hatem's drawings of a farting dragon, a two-headed cat, and stinky cheese.

# Join Yasmin on all her adventures!